Kestrels 5

The Stolen Pony

Kestrels 5

The Stolen Pony

Patricia Leitch

Illustrated by Elsie Lennox

Lions
An Imprint of HarperCollinsPublishers

First published in Great Britain in Lions in 1995

Lions is an imprint of Collins Children's Books,
a division of HarperCollinsPublishers Ltd, 77–85 Fulham
Palace Road, Hammersmith, London W6 8JB

1 3 5 7 9 10 8 6 4 2

Text copyright © Patricia Leitch 1995
Illustrations copyright © Elsie Lennox 1995

ISBN 0 00 674928 3

The author asserts the moral right to be identified
as the author of the work

Printed and bound in Great Britain
by HarperCollinsManufacturing Ltd, Glasgow

Chapter One

The beams of the spotlight turned the darkness of Mr Frazer's indoor school into a pool of harsh electric light. It was brighter than day. In the enclosed arena the red-and-white showjumps looked like objects from outer space. Sally Lorimer sat astride Willow, her dapple grey, Araby pony, and gazed at the jumps. They were terrifyingly high and the spread of poles seemed to Sally to leave no room for a pony to twist and turn and find its way over the maze of jumps.

Sally and her best friend Thalia (rhymes-with-dahlia-which-is-a-flower-like-a-chry-

santhemum) Nisbet were waiting to jump
in the charity Christmas horse show which
was held every year in the week between
Christmas and New Year at Mr Frazer's
indoor riding school. It had started as a
small local show but over the years it had
grown and grown, drawing many of the
best riders from the northwest of Scotland,
until now it was almost as big as Broughton
Show, one of the biggest horse shows in the
area.

"Absolutely brill!" exclaimed Thalia.
"This is the best bit, waiting to jump. Wish
you could buy it in a bottle and drink it
when you're bored."

Sally eased the brim of her hard hat, ran
her hand down Willow's hard neck and
tried to swallow but her mouth and throat
were brick-dry.

"It's not fair," she thought. "I'm not
good enough. The jumps are far too high. I
shouldn't be here. They'll laugh at Willow
and it will be my fault for mucking it up."

Sally was not tall, not small; not fat, not
skinny but sort of medium. Her thick
brown hair was cut in a fringe and grew

6

straight to her shoulders. She had wide-set blue eyes and a quirky mouth that turned up at the corners. She was ten years old and so was Thalia who was tall and lean with fizzing, corn-coloured hair and bright hazel-coloured eyes.

Thalia lived with her Narg, which is gran spelt backwards, in a tea-cosy cottage by the shore. Her parents were divorced. When they had split up Thalia had come to live with Narg and they had given her Tarquin, her almost thoroughbred, roan pony.

Sally lived with her family in Kestrels, a vast stone house with turrets and a tower. It was built on a peninsula of land, only joined to the mainland by a long, tree-lined drive – almost an island. There was a stable yard, with a range of stabling where both girls kept their ponies, and a well-fenced pony-field with a slow-flowing stream, a huge horse chestnut tree and an open-fronted shed for shelter.

The Lorimers had come to live there when Sally's father unexpectedly inherited a lot of money from his Great Uncle

Nathan. Kestrels was the house all Sally's family had dreamed of owning but without much hope until the letter from the solicitor arrived one magical morning.

Two boys were waiting with Sally and Thalia at one end of the indoor school. They would be the first to jump.

Both Willow and Tarquin had been specially groomed the night before for the Christmas Show but, while Willow looked clean and well cared for, Tarquin glimmered and glinted under the lights. He clinked his bit, his forefeet trampling into the yielding sand as he sank his weight on to his quarters, threatening to rear. He was as desperate as his rider to be soaring over the jumps.

Thalia sat securely in the saddle, completely at ease, her hands light on Tarquin's reins. She was longing to be out in the glare of the spotlights, facing the challenge of the painted jumps. She glanced at the shadowy rows of spectators and grinned to herself at the thought of their applause, which would surely follow her out of the ring after she had jumped.

An official-looking, grey-suited man walked towards the waiting children. It was about to begin.

"Number 34," he said, speaking to one of the boys. "You're first to jump. When you hear the whistle, ride into the ring and a steward will check your number and start you off. Keep alert, now. Be ready for your turn," and he strode away carrying his clipboard like a shield in front of him.

Almost immediately there was a sharp blast on the whistle, and the boy on his raw-boned chestnut rode into the ring. He had four jumps down.

"Beastly double," muttered Thalia to herself. "Need to keep wide after the wall."

Her whole attention was focused on the second boy. He rode a sharp, clear round on a bay pony.

The whistle blew again and it was Sally's turn.

"Please, please let it be all right," she prayed. "Don't let me come off. Don't let me make a fool of Willow."

She knew that, if she would only ride on at the jumps, Willow would clear them easily. Whatever went wrong would be her fault, and this seemed to make it much worse.

Sally gripped her reins tightly as Willow trotted into the arena. The spotlights dazzled. Willow pricked neat ears, looked round calmly through gentle eyes and stopped beside the steward who was waiting for Sally.

"Number 26?"

Sally nodded numbly.

"In your own time. When you're ready. Remember to ride through the Start. On you go. And don't worry about it. It's not the end of the world," the steward added, seeing Sally's strained expression.

Trotting through the Start, Sally was unbalanced and already clutching at Willow's mane. She hated the closed-in arena; had no idea which of the monstrous jumps she was meant to jump first. Half an hour ago, when she had walked round the jumps, they had all seemed quite different.

Vaguely she steered Willow at a red-and-white pole. She stood up in her stirrups and, hanging on to a clump of mane, she waited, frozen, while Willow flipped over the jump. She was badly left behind, had lost her stirrups, and seemed entangled in reins that were suddenly the length of skipping ropes.

Willow rose over crossed poles. Sally's nose banged into Willow's neck and, as Willow landed, Sally slid to the ground.

Stewards rushed towards her.

"I'm all right. I'm OK," Sally muttered, struggling to her feet while Willow waited, her hoofs primly planted in the sand and an expression of mild disdain on her face.

Cringing into herself Sally rode out of the ring. She had been disqualified for taking the wrong course. She had jumped the last jump first.

But it had happened. The worst had happened. It was past. The tightly clenched fist in Sally's stomach began to loosen its grip.

"Prime nit," scorned Thalia, but really she hardly saw Sally. All her being was fixed on the jumps and the tense energy of her pony.

Tarquin pranced in, rearing with impatience as Thalia gave her number to the steward and burst into a canter that changed to a gallop as they charged through the Start.

Thalia eased her fingers on the reins and, sitting close and neat over Tarquin's withers, soared over the first jump. The course she was to ride was as clear in Thalia's mind as if it had been marked out with a red carpet. Seeming to do nothing, Thalia rode Tarquin over the jumps. Rider and pony were so close that Tarquin responded to the slightest touch on his reins, the least tightening of Thalia's leg on his side. Speed was their element – to gallop and soar and gallop again.

The grin on Thalia's face stretched from ear to ear as Tarquin cleared the spread of poles that was the last jump. In two galloping strides they were through the Finish. They had jumped a clear round. The spectators let out their breath and clapped furiously.

Riding out of the indoor school into the stable yard, Thalia leapt to the ground and flung her arms round Tarquin's neck.

"Well," said Martine Dawes, who was Mr Frazer's head riding instructor. "That was some exhibition."

Although she disapproved of Thalia's wild speed she couldn't keep a note of excitement from creeping into her voice and, when Thalia looked up, Martine was smiling at her.

Mr Frazer's was a posh riding school. Sally and Thalia knew Martine well. She had given them lessons and driven them and their ponies to Pony Club events. She rode a black thoroughbred, and both Sally and Thalia thought she was terrific.

"But they're all fantastic riders," Sally thought miserably, looking round the mushrooming horseboxes, floats and trailers that had sprung up in the fields surrounding Mr Frazer's indoor school. "And they all saw me falling off!"

"That boy went clear, didn't he?" Martine asked. "So there'll be a jump-off. Loosen Tarquin's girth and lift his saddle.

Lead him about for a few minutes to cool down, then tighten your girth and ride him around again. Don't want him to lose interest. Let him know that he has to jump again."

Suddenly Tarquin flung up his head and sent his brazen whinny bannering out over horses and humans, challenging them all.

"Of course he knows he has to jump again!" stated Thalia.

There were two more clear rounds, which made four for the jump-off. Martine found a stall where Sally could leave Willow while they both watched Thalia jumping. Two of the riders had faults. Thalia and the boy who had jumped before her went clear.

"Let's hope they share first prize," said Martine, "or she'll be in orbit!"

"Ladies and gentlemen," announced the loudspeaker. "We have a tie for first place. There will be a jump-off against the clock."

"Glory!" exclaimed Martine. "No point in telling her to steady up now."

Chapter Two

Sally dug her nails into the palms of her hands willing the boy to crash through the jumps, but the boy, riding confidently into the ring, had no intention of knocking anything down. His bay was as fast as Tarquin, spinning on the spot, twisting and turning. He was clear.

"And a time of only sixty-five seconds."

Applause drowned the announcer's voice.

Sally wanted to close her eyes so that she didn't have to look, but she couldn't. Her whole attention was fixed on Tarquin and Thalia.

At the sound of the whistle Tarquin reared, then leapt forward through the Start. Thalia urged him on. Over crossed poles, the brush, the wall, the spread of poles, he flowed like water with the speed of flame.

Where the boy had ridden a jagged round, pulling his pony back on its hocks, kicking it on, dominating it, Thalia had hardly moved. The same joy ran through Tarquin and herself. They were only wrong once. At the double they came in too close. The spectators' gasp seemed to come from a single throat.

Tarquin cat-jumped over the first part, touched down, stretched out and cleared the second part, jumping at an angle so he was ready to clear the final jump and race, low to the ground, through the Finish.

"Her time? Her time?" Martine shouted.

"Sixty-one seconds," triumphed the loudspeaker.

Martine clapped her hands above her head and stamped her feet, while Sally wrapped her arms round herself in case she should explode with excitement.

They watched as Thalia was presented with a red-and-gold First rosette, then raced round to meet Thalia in the yard.

"He was super! Wasn't he super?" cried Thalia, trotting to meet them. Her squidgy, mulberry-coloured hard hat which she had worn for years, so that now it was more a soft hat than a hard hat, was in her hand, setting her hair free to halo her head. "Wasn't he super? Super-great. He's the best showjumping pony in the world!'

And it wasn't conceit. It wasn't boasting. It was sheer joy that her pony had jumped so well.

"You weren't too bad yourself," said Martine.

"Not too fast?" said Thalia, tongue in cheek.

Sally went to get Willow, pausing for a moment before she rejoined the others, to clap her neck, rub under her mane and give her a sweet from her jodhpur pocket.

"Was not your fault," she told her pony. "It was me for being so stupid," but Willow didn't care, all she wanted was to get back to Tarquin.

Total strangers congratulated Thalia. Mrs Blair, their Pony Club District Commissioner, came up to praise Tarquin and tell Thalia how well she had ridden.

"And what went wrong with you?" she asked Sally. "Willow would have popped over those jumps, and after you did so well at our one-day event."

"Perhaps Willow was dazzled by the lights," suggested Martine comfortingly, but Sally knew it was only an excuse.

A tall man with a black beard and a shock of grey hair, who seemed to know Martine, appeared at Tarquin's shoulder and asked if the pony was for sale. He said he knew a lassie who was looking for a pony with a bit of a jump in it that would take her to the top.

"You haven't a chance," laughed Martine.

"Sell Tarquin!" Thalia cried in amazement. "Of course he's not for sale. Never, never, *never* would I sell Tarquin!" and she threw her arms round Tarquin's neck to protect him.

"Don't you be so hasty now. Perhaps when your parents hear the rustle of pound notes, things could be different."

Thalia swung Tarquin round, barging her pony's quarters into the man, hurrying Tarquin away.

"He's a dealer from Radford. Bit of a chancer," said Martine following Tarquin, as the man walked away to find his horse-box. "We've had one or two nice ponies from him but you've got to watch him."

"Peugh!'" exclaimed Thalia when they caught up with her. "I couldn't bear to look at him. As if I'd sell Tarquin. A super showjumper like Tarquin! And he's mine. Parents! I don't have any parents! But I've got Tarquin and that's all that matters!"

"You've got our family," said Sally. "You're one of us."

Thalia hardly ever mentioned her divorced parents and now she only shrugged her shoulders as if it didn't really matter at all.

"I suppose this will mean you'll both be coming to Broughton Show?" asked Martine in a changing-the-subject tone of voice. "Thalia to show them that today wasn't just luck, and Sally to prove that today was nothing but bad luck."

"Broughton Show?" shouted Thalia, all

thoughts of parents or family totally wiped out of her mind, as totally as if they had never existed. To win a rosette at Broughton Show would be something pretty good.

"But you said we weren't good enough for Broughton. You said that you hadn't room for us in the box. That you couldn't take us!"

"The Baxter girls have mumps. When they recover they are being taken on a Mediterranean cruise. You two can take their places. Mr Frazer can change the entries for the class."

"Oh, thank you," cried Thalia, her eyes brilliant with happiness.

Sally made her mouth say the correct things, but she didn't want to go. Broughton was an indoor show. There would be blinding spotlights and the terrifying dazzle of jumps. She should say it now, tell them now that she was not going. As Sally felt in her jacket pocket, searching for a tissue, her hand closed on her crystal unicorn, her magic unicorn.

*   *   *

Just before her father had received the solicitor's letter telling him that Great Uncle Nathan had died and he had inherited the money that had bought Kestrels, and Willow, and paid for Sally's riding lessons, the Lorimers had been for a picnic at Fintry Bay close to Kestrels. Sally had been standing at the sea's edge when something glinting in the water had caught her eye. She had crouched down to see it more clearly and the slow frothing of a wave had carried a tiny crystal unicorn into Sally's outstretched hand and laid it in the very centre of her palm.

All day Sally had forgotten about her unicorn. That morning she had taken the unicorn from her bedroom windowsill and put it in her jacket pocket to bring her luck, but she had forgotten all about it.

"Bet you I wouldn't have fallen off if I'd remembered about it," Sally thought.

"I'll see Mr Frazer about Broughton," Martine said and it was too late for Sally to tell them that she wasn't going. "Must let Tarquin have his chance."

"What shall we do now?" Thalia asked when Martine had left them.

"Kestrels," said Sally.

It wasn't like a summer outdoor show. You couldn't ride around looking at things and chatting. Although it was only three o'clock, heavy clouds were piling up, darkening the already grey sky.

"OK," agreed Thalia.

They rode together, first along the deserted shore and then, to escape from the wind, up over the sand dunes and along the road to Kestrels.

Thalia tried to find out what had gone wrong with Sally's jumping.

"You didn't even know the course," she said.

"I did," said Sally, defending herself. "But when I got into the ring everything went wrong. It all looked different."

"It was you," Thalia insisted. "Honestly, Willow would have taken you over the jumps. Not like Tarquin, of course, but she would have jumped. *You* messed it up."

Sally glared at Thalia.

"I didn't mean—" she began, but Thalia was back in the ring again reliving the speed and the glamour of her round against the clock. "Did you see how he sorted himself out at the double? I was all wrong. Any other pony would have stopped but he didn't even think about it. He was mercury."

An icy blast of wind stung sleet into the back of their necks and made their ponies scuttle suddenly forward.

"Let's trot," said Sally. "Get home before it starts."

"Right," agreed Thalia, the scarlet-and-gold rosette still flaunting from Tarquin's bridle.

They trotted on until the long avenue leading down to Kestrels came into sight, then they steadied their ponies to a walk. As they reached the tree-lined avenue, they stopped before turning right. A car was coming up behind them. Not an ordinary, factory kind of car but the sort that people kept for a pet and drove for fun, or towed behind their everyday car taking it to rallies. Not quite an old crock, but almost.

It chugged past them, empty except for the small, balding man who was driving.

"Clear now," said Sally turning Willow to ride down the avenue to where Kestrels waited, welcoming her back with lighted windows.

Soon she would be at home with her family – her librarian father; her mother who believed that only dull women had superclean houses, and much preferred to spend her time painting in watercolours or walking the dogs; her sixteen-year-old brother, Ben, who lived in a world of books; Emma, her sister, who was thirteen, had long fair hair and overflowed with singing and dancing; and the youngest Lorimer, Jamie, who was just five.

Sally let the thought of her disastrous day slip to the back of her mind. Her parents would understand.

They had almost reached Kestrels before Sally noticed Thalia's silence. She glanced back and, even in the deadening light, she could see that something was wrong with Thalia.

"Are you all right?" Sally called.

"Fine," Thalia answered, but her voice was clenched, her face white and her lips tucked in. She had taken the rosette off Tarquin's bridle. Its ribbons flagged from her jacket pocket.

"Are you sure?" demanded Sally.

The front door of Kestrels was flung open and the Lorimer dogs rushed out to welcome them. Fen flowed elegantly down the steps. She was a white hound with a fine, delicate head and strange, pale eyes. Misty, their light-grey and white Bearded Collie bustled down, a mass of beardie hair and two glowing, brown eyes. Meanwhile Meg, their black-and-white Beardie, who was thirteen but doing very well on her heart pills, stood on the top step barking.

"Well, how did it go?" shouted Mr Lorimer.

"Did you win?" demanded Jamie, dancing beside his father. "Bet you won! Bet you won!"

"Need to give Tarquin a drink," muttered Thalia and she rode at a battering trot straight past Kestrels, ignoring dogs and Lorimers, and on to the stables.

"What's happened?" asked Mr Lorimer, but Sally had no idea.

Chapter Three

Mr Lorimer and Jamie followed Sally round to the stables. Thalia had already taken off Tarquin's tack, tied up his hay net and was rubbing him down, keeping her back turned to the door.

"Sally says you won. Good for you."

Thalia didn't look round.

Mr Lorimer paused, realizing that something must have upset Thalia, not quite knowing what to do.

"There's soup and baked potatoes waiting for you," he said. "Tell us all about it then."

He turned back to the house, swinging

Jamie by one hand in giant leaps.

"Brute of a wind," he called back. "I'll give you a run home to Narg's when you've finished your soup."

Normally, when Sally and Thalia came back from a show, they chatted together as they settled their ponies and then leant on the half-doors of the loose boxes, watching their ponies eating their feeds. But tonight was different. Thalia hardly spoke, more or less ignoring Sally. She tipped oats and pony nuts into Tarquin's trough, then swung round and bolted up the box door with hardly a word to Tarquin.

"I'm going now," she said to Sally.

"But your soup and spud? You must come in when Mum's made it for us. And to let them see your rosette."

"Haven't time. Narg will be waiting for me," and Thalia marched out of the stable yard towards the track that led down from Kestrels to the shore.

"Come back," shouted Sally racing after her. "Dad's going to drive you home."

"No!" shouted Thalia, not turning round or slowing down.

"Well, wait for me. I'll get the dogs and come with you, but wait. Wait!" yelled Sally.

She dashed back to Kestrels, into the kitchen and grabbed up Misty's and Fen's leads.

"Going to Narg's," Sally told her surprised family, and was running back over the winter-withered lawns and flowerbeds with the dogs leaping in front of her before they had time to ask any questions.

Thalia had waited. She was standing staring out at the waves as they rolled in over the sands. Grey sky, grey sea and grey, clay sand; only the gulls were glowing white against the storm clouds.

Thalia and Sally stomped their way towards Narg's without speaking. Questions buzzed in Sally's head but Thalia was hunched into herself and Sally knew she wouldn't answer. Then suddenly Thalia spoke.

"That man driving the old car was my dad," she said, and began to tell Sally about her parents' divorce.

"I think Mum and Dad were fed up with each other and fed up with me, too. They were always fighting about money – on and on and on. Dad would buy things, quite big things, like the time he bought the caravan and there was no money in the bank to pay for it, so they came the next day to take it back and all Mum's friends were at our house when they came, just as she was showing it to them. That was some row! He was always buying old cars and, when he hadn't paid the instalments, he would hide the letters and Mum would find them and that meant more fighting. Screaming at each other. I hid under the bedclothes but I could still hear them."

Sally listened in cold amazement. Nothing like that happened in her family. They were always the same, as the grass is always green.

"Dad works with computers. They have offices all over and when they opened a branch in Washington, in America, that made everything worse. Mum never knew what was going to happen next. Not even when he would be coming home. In the end they had to sell the house to pay off the bills. Mum and I came to live with Narg and after that they told me they were going to get a divorce. I didn't care because they gave me Tarquin. For ages I expected someone to turn up and take Tarquin away because he hadn't been paid for."

"But they didn't," said Sally. "He is yours now, isn't he?"

"You never know," said Thalia darkly. "Why is my dad here? Probably here to take Tarquin back and sell him."

"And where is your mum?" asked Sally, who had never liked to ask Thalia about her parents.

"She and Narg didn't get on too well, sharing the cottage and both of them trying to boss me, so she got a job with Oxfam in their London offices. Then she used to come to Narg's at the weekends, but after a bit she felt she had to go out and work with the children in Africa. Couldn't bear to think of all the suffering while all she was doing was sitting in a cosy, safe office. I know how she felt. I'd be the same. And she does write lots of letters to me.

Part of Tarquin is from Mum so he can't take him away from me. He can't." And Thalia hunched her shoulders and marched on.

As they got closer to the cottage perched above the shore, Sally saw that there was a car parked at Narg's front door. It was the old-fashioned car that had passed them just before they had reached Kestrels' drive.

"He's here," said Thalia. "He's blooming well come! I thought that perhaps he might just have been driving through. He can't have known it was me or he'd have stopped. I would have thought that he wouldn't want to go near Narg. But, he's here all right," and Thalia drew down her brows and scowled furiously in the direction of the vintage car.

"Yes. I bet you he's here to take Tarquin. He'll have no money. He'll be here to see if he can get Tarquin and sell him."

"He wouldn't!" exclaimed Sally. In her wildest nightmare she could never imagine her father selling Willow.

"He could," said Thalia darkly. "You've

32

no idea what he's like when he's got no money. Take anything and sell it. Took Mum's engagement ring once and sold it. That's what he's like.

"Come on. Let's get it over with," and, quickening her pace, Thalia raced up the steps to Narg's.

Sally hardly had time to catch Fen and Misty before Thalia had bashed the back door open and burst into the raftered living room. Sally hurried behind her.

Narg was sitting in her usual armchair; opposite her, on the other side of the hearth, sat a small man in a grey suit. His face was smooth, his sparse, sandy hair was carefully arranged over his bald head and his grey eyes were like wet pebbles, totally without expression.

"Darling," he said in a light voice, greeting Thalia. "How you have grown. Daddy would hardly have known you." He got out of his chair and was about to put his arms round Thalia when he drew back. "But you're soaking, dear. Absolutely filthy. Do go and change. Then we can have a little chat.

"Does she often come in soaking wet like this?" he asked, turning to Narg. "It can't be good for her. And her boots are utterly disgusting. Shouldn't she be leaving this kind of thing behind, now she's . . . How old are you, dear?"

"Doesn't even know his own daughter's age," thought Sally, hardly able to believe her ears. Already she was quite certain that she did not like Thalia's father. Did not like him in the least.

Thalia stood glowering at her father. "Why are you here?" she demanded.

"To see you, of course,"

Thalia snorted in disbelief. "You're not having Tarquin. You both promised. He's mine. You can't take him. I've got it written down and you both signed it."

"What nonsense is this? Take your pony? Whatever would I do with a pony?"

"You'd sell him, if you've no money. If you're here looking for money, you'd take him and sell him. You wouldn't care."

"My dear Thalia. I assure you," stated Mr Nisbet, "I am here to see *you*. I've been at our office in Denburgh so I thought I'd

34

nip across. See how you're getting on and spend a day or two with you. I wouldn't dream of taking your pony."

"Yes you would! Oh yes you would!"

Narg roused herself, and stood up. "Better take those boots off,' she said to Thalia. "Go and get changed and we'll have something to eat. How about Sally? Are you staying?"

Sally shook her head. She was standing behind the settee, as if it could protect her from Thalia's rage. Clutching the dogs' leads she was almost afraid of Thalia and her father, of the temper that had flared up so suddenly between them, filling Narg's safe, cosy room with fury.

"Scrambed eggs?" Narg offered, but Mr Nisbet gave his mouth smile and said he was going to take them both out for dinner, that was if Thalia could make herself fit to be seen.

"I'd better go," said Sally. "My family will be wondering what's happened to me."

Misty, hearing the word "go", did vertical take-offs at the end of her lead, aiming at Sally's face.

"OK," said Thalia. "Look in at Tarquin. Just in case. I'll be round tomorrow, first thing."

"Oh no. No," said her father. "I've planned a day out. No mothers-in-law, only the two of us. We're going to Creswell Zoo, so Thalia won't be coming out to play tomorrow."

"Play!" exploded Thalia. "I shall be at Kestrels. I've got to see to Tarquin. Make sure he's not stiff after today. And I am NOT, am never, NOT, going near a zoo. They are yeuch, double-yeuch places."

Sally let the dogs pull her out of the room. Thalia followed her to the back door.

"I'll see you tomorrow," she said loudly. "As if I'd ever leave Tarquin with him about!"

Sally was telling her disbelieving family about Thalia's father when the phone rang. Mr Lorimer answered it.

"Yes," he said. "Rob Lorimer here."

Although Sally listened intently she could not make out who was speaking.

"No problem at all. I'm certain we can cope with Tarquin for one day," said Mr Lorimer.

"Thalia's father," guessed Sally.

"Well, that's true," said Mr Lorimer, speaking into the phone. "But it's the stage they're at. Sally is exactly the same. Thinks of nothing but Willow. We're only too happy to have Thalia around the place. Good company for Sally."

There was a long silence while Mr Lorimer listened.

"Well, that is one way of looking at it," Mr Lorimer said, so that Sally knew he didn't agree with whatever it was that Mr Nisbet had been saying.

Mr Lorimer put the phone down and, shrugging his shoulders, he turned to his family. "Thalia's dad. He's taking her to a museum and a heritage park tomorrow so she won't be here. We are to attend to his lordship. And he feels you should both be encouraged to take an interest in other things. Spend less time with your ponies."

Chapter Four

Next morning, when Sally went down to the stables, there was a note from Thalia pinned on the door of Tarquin's box.

"He's kidnapped me. Guard Tarquin with your life – Thalia. PS Not an animal-torture prison but a museum. Stuffed, not suffering."

"I'll stay down here all day with the dogs and a showjumping book," Sally told Willow as she mucked out. "You're quite safe. It's Tarquin he's after."

Sally didn't know whether to believe Thalia or not. Would her father really sell Tarquin? Wanting Thalia to be more grown-up was one thing but she couldn't honestly think that anyone's father would sell his daughter's pony without explaining the terrible necessity that was making him do it. And today he was really only taking Thalia out for the day, not exactly kidnapping her.

When she had fed the ponies, Sally brushed them over, carefully inspecting them in case there were any scratches or bruises from yesterday. They were both fine.

Sally tacked up Tarquin and led him round the yard while he pranced at the length of his reins, his head high as he winnied for Thalia. There was not the slightest sign of stiffness.

"Well, I'm missing her, too," Sally told him as she tightened his girth. "Now stand still until I get up."

As Sally gathered up her reins, putting her foot in the stirrup, there was a sudden coldness in the pit of her stomach. It was Tarquin she was going to ride, not Willow; Tarquin who, the first time she had ridden him, had run away with her.

For a moment, in Sally's fearful imagination, Tarquin seemed a sixteen-hand hunter; too strong for Sally to ride, too high for her to mount without someone to hold him for her. Sally looked round despairingly, hoping that Ben or Emma might appear. But there was no sign of any Lorimer. Sally went on hopping at Tarquin's side.

"Go on," she told herself. "Don't be such a wet. What would Thalia say if she could see you? Laugh like a drain," and, gritting her teeth, Sally jumped and squirmed into the saddle. She gathered up her reins, steadying Tarquin to a striding, spring-heeled walk, and rode him past Kestrels and down the long avenue, between the bare beech trees.

"Enjoy. Enjoy," Sally commanded herself and rode on, appreciating Tarquin's electric energy.

Never in a million years would Sally have exchanged Willow for Tarquin but, now she was riding him, she understood why Thalia was so proud of him. Sitting on Tarquin, Sally felt as if she could have jumped any spread of poles or any red-and-white wall. Tarquin would have cleared it effortlessly.

When Sally had exercised Willow, she put her back in her box and gave each pony an extra armful of hay.

"I'll be back to turn you out when I've had some juice,' she promised them and hurried back to Kestrels, feeling important and in charge of things – head groom in a racing stable.

"Martine phoned," called her mother. "Invitation for you to go over this afternoon and ride in their indoor school. I said, Yes, you'd love to go. You've to be there for two."

"But I can't. I have to look after the ponies. I can't possibly go."

"Look after the ponies? They'll be in their field, won't they?"

"Yes, of course, but I promised Thalia I'd watch Tarquin extra specially."

Sally stared at her mother blankly, her free day of pretending to be a girl groom suddenly snatched away from her; her nerves twitched by fear of having to jump in Mr Frazer's indoor school.

"I don't want—" began Sally.

"Have some orange, and there's crisps. I'll come down with you, give you a hand with their New Zealand rugs and we'll put them both out for a bit."

At half past one Sally was riding Willow along the shore to Mr Frazer's. Her mother, realizing that Sally was worried about leaving Tarquin alone, had promised to take her painting things out to the stable and spend the afternoon there. Tarquin would be perfectly safe.

"Wonder what Thalia's doing," said Sally, urging Willow on into the wind. "She would be furious if she knew I was having a lesson with Martine. But me . . .? I only want to ride you round about Kestrels. That's what I enjoy."

The trouble was that it was not true. Deep down Sally desperately wanted to jump as well as Thalia and, since this was what she truly wanted, there was nothing else to do but to get on with it.

The private pupil looked about fourteen. She was mounted on Blossom, Mr Frazer's steadiest cob, so Sally knew that she wasn't a fantastic rider.

"I'm Hannah. Glad you've come," the girl said, smiling at Sally. "It means that Martine's eagle eye will not be on me all the time."

Martine switched on the spotlights and closed the sliding doors of the indoor school.

"May as well have the full effect," she said. "Now ride round, keep well out to the edge of the school. Let your ponies settle. Relax. I'm not going to eat you. Well, not yet."

As they walked and trotted round the indoor school Sally began to feel at home. Inside there was nothing to distract Willow. She was paying complete attention to Sally; asking "What next?" as she went round at a balanced trot, ears alert and eyes bright.

"This is where we jumped in the show," Sally thought, hardly able to believe that it could possibly be the same place. The painted jumps that had terrified Sally were only the same jumps that had stood in the jumping paddock during the summer. Why had they seemed so huge and menacing at the show? Today there was masses of room in the ring; why had it seemed so small before?

"Idiot," Sally told herself, laughing aloud as Willow, cantering in a circle, popped over three small jumps.

Martine let them choose their own course round the showjumps; made them concentrate until they really knew the course they had chosen, then sent them out, one at a time, to ride round without jumping.

"It's a good thing to practise," she told them. "Or draw different showjumps on a sheet of paper, pick out your course, think about how you are going to take each jump, then, linking them together, ride round the course with your pencil. Your pony can't do its best for you if *you* don't know exactly how you mean to jump the course!"

Towards the end of the lesson Martine set up a simple course for them. She made them concentrate on how they were going to tackle the whole course. Then she sent Sally out to jump first.

"Throw your thoughts in front of you," she told Sally. "Horse of the Year next!"

Sally grinned.

"Thalia, not me," she said, but she was really enjoying herself; not pretending, not telling herself that she MUST enjoy jumping but truly, totally, having a good time.

"One pole down," said Martine. "And that was exactly the same course you made such a mess of before."

It was after five when Sally got home to Kestrels. Her mother had abandoned her post, but Tarquin was perfectly safe. The yard was full of Emma and the dogs.

"I've done Tarquin," said Em, coming out of Tarquin's box. "Only three attempts to grab him, but Misty saw them off."

"Hope you didn't let the dogs in the boxes," said Sally, ignoring her sister's teasing. "They pee everywhere and then the ponies won't lie down."

"Never noticed," said Emma. "Expect you're fussing as usual."

"No," said Sally. "Martine told us."

As they walked across the tussocky, neglected grass that might one day be lawn, the dogs spread out in front of them, Fen ranging ahead, stopping suddenly and leaping round to come, like a gazelle, stretched out with speed, to bound around them before she raced away again.

Misty sniffled and rolled and shook her long coat to free it from twigs, dead leaves and mud. When she shook herself she planted her muffed paws foursquare on the ground and bushed out the strands of her coat into a feather duster, her eyes closed to slits and her nose pointed.

Meg plodded sedately at their side. When Meg stopped, Sally and Em stopped too, waiting for her.

"And I was jumping round the course just like Thalia," Sally told Emma. "Sort of knowing in my head exactly where I was going."

"Sounds promising," said Emma.

"More than," said Sally. "But it would have been better if Thalia had been there. Do you think she'll be home? I'd better phone."

Narg said that Thalia was not home and she did not know when to expect them.

"That is the sixth time you have phoned," Sally's mother told her, as Sally wandered innocently in the direction of the telephone.

It was well after ten and Sally had only managed to stay up so late by sitting silently in a corner, scratching Meg and reading.

"I must tell her that Tarquin is safely locked in his box," Sally insisted. "That her father hasn't stolen him."

"How could he, when he was with Thalia?" demanded Ben from the depths of *The Sword in the Stone*.

"He could have fixed it," said Sally darkly.

"Leave a message," said Sally's father. "This is positively the last phone call."

Narg felt the same. "Isn't it time you were in bed?" she said sharply. "You'll see Thalia in the morning."

Next morning Sally and her family and all the dogs heard Thalia before they saw her.

"Sally. Sally!" Thalia yelled at the pitch of her powerful lungs, from where she stood below Sally's window. "Sally! I'm back!"

"Shut her up," roared Mr Lorimer but Sally was already out of bed and pushing up her bedroom window. "Dad says you've to shut up. I'll come and let you in."

Sally galloped down the flights of Kestrels' stairs, told the dogs to belt up as she raced through the kitchen and unlocked the door.

"Tarquin?" she demanded urgently.

"OK. I've seen him. He's fine," and Thalia, looking as if she hadn't even brushed her hair, marched into the kitchen. "I know," she said. "I'm disgustingly early but I had to see Tarquin and I did wake up the dogs, but that only proves what super watchdogs they are.

"We've got to go for a long ride. Now. At once. Dad is going today, so if I can keep out of his sight until he's away, Tarquin will be safe."

"Did your dad say anything about selling Tarquin?"

"Didn't give him a chance. I talked all the time. Think he was pretty fed up with me by the time we got back to Narg's."

"One might say you are rather early," Mrs Lorimer said, drifting into the kitchen to make coffee. "Does Narg know you're here?"

"I left her a note," said Thalia. "We're going for a long ride, that's why I'm a bit early. Shall we go to Montreith loch? You can see for miles once you get up there, and I've got sandwiches. Dad'll have gone by the time we get back."

"What is all this silly nonsense about your father?" asked Mrs Lorimer, putting a bowl of flakes in front of Thalia. "I'm quite sure he wouldn't dream of selling Tarquin."

"Would he not? He sure would. 'By the way, your mother and I have decided to get divorced.' 'By the way, you are going to live with Narg.' 'By the way, I've decided to sell your pony.' That's how he does things."

In spite of Thalia's urgency, it was after nine before they were trotting down the avenue away from Kestrels. High above them, patches of blue sky grew between the vanishing clouds. A luminous sun glowed through drifting mists and a frosting of snow glittered on the hilltops. It was going to be a blue day. Only the wind was as vicious as ever.

"If we're going to Montreith we have to ride past Narg's," Sally said, when they reached the road. Although she had never ridden to Montreith loch before, she had been there several times in the car.

Thalia brought Tarquin to a halt. Her mind was fixed on riding to Montreith, on eating her doorstep sandwiches sitting on a boulder by the loch. Once Thalia had seen otters there. "Doesn't matter," she decided. "*He* won't be up yet."

They turned right and trotted on into the wind. The bright day, the thought of Thalia's father and the excitement of riding to Montreith sent a sudden shudder down Sally's spine.

Mr Nisbet's car was still parked at Narg's as they walked past on the grass verge to muffle the ponies' hoofbeats.

"Freedom!" shouted Thalia and she urged Tarquin into a canter, not seeing the curtain pulled back in Narg's bedroom window and her father looking out.

Tarquin, not expecting the sudden burst of speed, humped his back and bucked, changing from a canter to a full-out gallop. His mane and tail fanned out in the wind.

"On you go," yelled Thalia, giving Tarquin his head. "We're free! He can't get you now," and she urged her pony on.

When at last she steadied him and turned back to Sally, Tarquin was shying and dancing, tossing his head and jangling his bit, his hoofs prancing as he danced on fire.

He refused to walk; even when they trotted on, he refused to settle. He shied at the least thing. A plastic bag blowing across the road made him rear wildly. Goggle-eyed he fought Thalia, wanting only to gallop again.

"He is pure brill when he's like this," Thalia rejoiced.

To reach Montreith they had to ride for about half an hour along a much busier road. There were plans to change it into a dual carriageway, but so far nothing had been done and the road that had been built for a few vans or lorries now shuddered under the weight of articulated monsters and gigantic crate-carriers.

"Single file," said Sally, wishing that this bit of the ride was over and they were walking up the heathery track to the loch.

Keeping well in, close to the stone walls of the superior bungalows that edged the road, Sally and Thalia rode towards Montreith. Even Willow hated it, and only Thalia's riding kept Tarquin going forward.

"It's much, much worse than the last time I rode along here," Thalia shouted back to Sally.

Sally's reply was drowned by the sudden pumping of a car horn close behind them. The noise blared through the traffic's roar.

"Dad," shrieked Thalia in dismay, as they both looked back to see who was making such a din.

"Look out," screamed Sally in horror, but Thalia was too shocked by the sight of her father's car to be aware of the lorry coming towards them on the other side of the road.

It was loaded with wooden crates which

should have been roped down under a green tarpaulin but the ropes had come undone and the tarpaulin flapped free, billowing into the air, mopping and mowing as the wind filled it, making it leap high above the cab of the lorry. Like some fiend of the air, the lorry bore down upon them while, just behind them, Mr Nisbet blasted his horn.

Chapter Five

Willow's stirrup struck against the stone wall as she sprang away from the lorry. She tripped, plunging her nose into the mud, almost tipping Sally out of the saddle. Sally hardly noticed, all her attention was fixed on Thalia and Tarquin. As if it was a film Sally could only watch, could do nothing.

Tarquin reared up, balancing on air, touched down, his front shoes scoring the road before he reared again, even higher. Sally saw Thalia's hat fall off, bounce on to Tarquin's quarters, making Tarquin panic into the path of the oncoming traffic. There was the screaming of brakes, the skid of tyres as traffic screeched to a halt. The tarpaulin cracked above Tarquin's head. Trying to escape from it, Tarquin took one galloping stride between the cars, lost his balance and crashed to the ground. Thalia was thrown clear.

For a split second Tarquin lay absolutely still, then he fought to find a footing to lift himself up. Sally flung herself off Willow, still clutching her reins she tried to reach Tarquin, but she was too late. Tarquin plunged upright – bucking, galloping, reins and stirrups flying, he raced away between the lines of traffic while Thalia lay where she had fallen – motionless, only her yellow hair blowing against the road.

Car doors were flung open. Strangers rushed to Thalia. Her father came, quick and nervous, kneeling down by Thalia but not knowing what to do. A woman, pushing her way through the group of people who had gathered round Thalia, said she was a doctor. Efficiently she checked Thalia's pulse, lifted her eyelids and loosened her clothes. A man who had run out of one of the bungalows asked if he should ring for an ambulance.

"Yes," said the doctor, "and tell them that it's urgent."

Someone brought a car rug and covered Thalia.

"Don't move her," warned the doctor.

A police car appeared from nowhere and the policemen organized the traffic into motion again.

Sally leant against the bungalow wall, her arm over Willow's neck. She couldn't stop her teeth chattering and tears trickling down her face. She blew her nose hard and told herself not to be so stupid, for of course Thalia was not dead. She had only banged her head; was only unconscious.

It took the ambulance almost twenty minutes to reach them but no one paid any attention to Sally. It wasn't until two white-coated men had lifted Thalia on to a stretcher, loaded her into the ambulance and driven her away, followed by Thalia's father in his car, that a policeman came over to speak to Sally.

"Did you see the accident?" he asked in a

tone of voice that made it sound most unlikely. "Shouldn't you be getting home, not hanging around here?"

"I was with Thalia," Sally replied in a high, strained voice.

"Were you now? Andy, here's a lassie says she was riding with the casualty."

The other policeman came over and they took down all that Sally could tell them.

"They've taken her to Carterhill Infirmary. Tell your parents to phone, and find out how she is."

Sally nodded.

"You're sure you'll be all right now, riding home by yourself? We'll drive in front of you if you like?"

"No. Honestly. I often ride by myself. I'm fine."

"If you are really sure," said the policeman, half of his attention on a message that was coming through on his radio. "Go straight home. We'll be in touch with your parents." And the two policemen drove away.

Willow was grazing by the roadside at

the length of her reins. Sally pulled her head up and mounted.

"Got to get home and find out how Thalia is," Sally said, turning Willow to ride back to Kestrels. She was waiting for a break in the traffic when suddenly she remembered.

"Tarquin!" she cried aloud. "We all forgot about Tarquin!"

Guilt flooded over Sally. What would Thalia think? What if Tarquin has been hurt or fallen again? How was it possible that no one had said anything about Tarquin? Then Sally remembered that she had forgotten about him herself. They had all been too concerned about Thalia.

As Sally trotted urgently in the direction that Tarquin had taken, she pictured him dragging a broken leg or lying by the side of the road bleeding to death.

No one had seen any sign of a runaway pony. People she asked looked at her suspiciously, as if she were looking for a runaway rhinoceros and not a pony.

She seemed to have been searching for ages when she stopped by a farm track, trying to think what she should do next. She couldn't go on like this. She could easily have missed Tarquin. He could be any-where, shocked and hurt. Suddenly Sally remembered her unicorn. She felt in her jacket pocket, brought it out and it lay in her hand, sparkling in a sudden glint of sunlight.

"I'll take it into hospital for Thalia," she thought.

A man came out of the farm door, raised his arm, shouted and came striding up to Sally.

"It's the day for the ponies," the farmer said. "You'll be the second one who has come to visit me this morning. The first one came calling on his own."

"A roan pony?" cried Sally.

"It is."

"Then it's Tarquin! Is he all right?"

"Going by the speed he's wrapping him-self round my hay, I'd say there's not much troubling him."

Sally and Willow hurried after the farmer and there was Tarquin sharing a hay barn with four calves. Abandoning Willow, Sally squeezed between the metal poles and ran to Tarquin.

"Tarquin!" she yelled. "I've found you. Oh Tarquin, you could have been killed!"

Tarquin knew Sally at once. Wuffling through wide nostrils he trotted towards her.

"We'll need to tell Thalia that you're safe," Sally told Tarquin, as he breathed over her. "She'll be more worried about you than anything else."

Sally told the farmer about the accident.

"Damned lucky it wasn't worse. That road's a disgrace, the traffic that's on it!" he said. "I'll be sending in my bill for the hay he's eaten."

"Which is impossible, for he doesn't know my address," Sally thought as, riding Willow and leading Tarquin, she trotted back to Kestrels. "We'll take him some chocolates," she decided and imagined herself and Thalia riding out to the farm under blue skies, surrounded by spring-green fields.

But . . .

It might not happen. There might be no Thalia. Sally urged the ponies on. She had to see Thalia; had to see for herself that she was all right; had to tell her that Tarquin was safe.

There was a note on the kitchen table.

Had to take Narg to the hospital. Phoned Mrs Blair. She's coming over. Phone vet at once if you need him. I hope *you're* OK. Back soon.
All my love, Mum XXX

Mrs Blair was the Pony Club District Commissioner. She was sturdy and capable. After years of Pony Club life, nothing to do with children and ponies could shake her.

Mrs Blair arrived minutes after Sally had finished reading her mother's note.

"What hat was she wearing?" Mrs Blair asked as she strode briskly down to the stables with Sally.

"It fell off."

"So it was that plum pudding she *will* insist on wearing. Crazy child! Now the elastic has rotted away, there's nothing to keep it on her head!"

Mrs Blair looked Tarquin over carefully. He had a long scratch on his off hind leg and a graze on his off shoulder.

"You were lucky, my lad," Mrs Blair said, as she bathed his injuries. "Could have been a broken leg and then what?"

Leaving the ponies in their boxes, they went back to Kestrels. Mrs Lorimer was just getting out of her car.

"How is she?" asked Mrs Blair.

"Still unconscious. She's to have a scan and that will let them see if there is any damage to her brain. Narg and Thalia's father are waiting to hear the result. They'll phone us whenever there's any news."

"She'll bounce up," Mrs Blair reassured them. "When you've seen as many kids as I have, splattered on the ground one minute and back in the saddle the next, you stop worrying about them."

But as they sat round the kitchen table questioning Sally about what had actually happened, they all knew it wasn't as simple as that.

Sally didn't feel hungry for lunch. She sat at the foot of Kestrels' curving staircase cuddled up to Meg and waited for the phone to ring. People phoned who had heard about the accident. Each time Sally's heart banged in her throat as she dashed to answer it but it was never Narg.

It was not until Sally came back from doing the ponies that Narg phoned.

"Nothing showed up on the scan," she told Mrs Lorimer. "No bleeding, so that's a relief. She's still unconscious and they're a bit concerned about that. I'm at home now, but I'm going in again tonight. Could you and Sally come too? They think Sally might just be able to reach her. It would only be for a few minutes but there's a chance that she might hear Sally."

"Of course I'll bring Sally. How are you getting in?"

"Her father is still here. He'll take me in to the hospital, then he's flying to Washington to some top-level conference that he must attend, so if I could come back with you? Wish we'd never seen the wretched man. Causes nothing but aggro. And why he had to go chasing off after Thalia like that, I do not know."

Car headlights swathed the darkness and, as they reached Carterhill, neon signs, lighted shop windows and traffic lights created a coruscating world of dazzle. Mrs Lorimer was concentrating on her driving, on finding the way to the hospital, while Sally sat next to her with her arms wrapped round herself. Yet it was only Thalia they were going to see. No need to be frightened of Thalia. Her best friend. Thalia. Sally clenched her teeth. Thalia would be all right. Just be herself.

Mrs Lorimer gave a sigh of relief as she swung the car into the hospital car park.

"We made it," she said. "Have you got the chocolates?"

Sally had, and a handful of hairs from Tarquin's mane and her unicorn to give to Thalia. She buried them deep in her pocket. She had a feeling that doctors or nurses might not approve of pony hairs being left with patients.

In the brilliantly lit reception area of the hospital Mrs Lorimer asked where they would find Thalia. She was in intensive care. They were to take a lift to the seventh floor and ask there if it would be possible to see her.

It was a shiny metal lift crammed tight

with people who all looked ill and un-happy, their reflections gathered around them like pallid ghosts. Sally reached for her mother's hand. This wasn't a place for Thalia. How could she get better in a place like this?

Narg was waiting for them at the nursing station.

"I've been with her for ten minutes. Her dad's in with her just now. I've had a word with Sister and she says it will be all right for you to go in together. Only a few min-utes, mind. You're to talk quietly to her. Nothing that will worry her. Best not to mention the accident and Sister says not to mention Tarquin in case it troubles her."

"But she'll want to know about Tarquin. To know he isn't hurt. I must tell her that."

"You can tell her when she comes round," said the Sister, coming up behind them on rubber-soled shoes. "For tonight, just let her know you're here."

Mr Nisbet came towards them down the long, fluorescent corridor. He was walking uncertainly, smoothing his thin hair over his scalp, glimpsing at his reflection in the glass walls of the corridor, twitching at his tie and coat sleeves.

"About five minutes," the Sister warned them as she took them to Thalia's room. "Remember we don't know whether she can hear us or not, so don't say anything to each other that you wouldn't want Thalia to hear," and the Sister pushed open a glass-panelled door and let Sally and her mother in.

Thalia lay flat on the bed. Her hair had been tied back and her face had been washed too much. She had a fine tube down her nose, rubber discs attached to wires were stuck on to her chest. Somehow, Sally couldn't quite make out how, everything seemed to join up to some sort of machine. Luminous green lights flickered and zigzagged across a computer screen. The bleeps of light were the only sign that Thalia was still alive.

Sally sat down on a chair at the far side of the bed. She listened to her mother telling Thalia how pleased they were to see her, that she was looking fine, that soon she would wake up and they would have a party at Kestrels when she came home.

Sally couldn't think of anything to say. It wasn't true that Thalia was looking fine. Sally could hear the falseness in her mother's voice and, if Thalia could hear, she would know that she must be looking dreadful.

Mrs Lorimer paused several times, giving Sally a chance to speak, but Sally avoided her eyes. She couldn't speak to Thalia without telling her about Tarquin. She could hardly believe that this girl lying on the bed could really be Thalia; Thalia who was never still for a minute; Thalia who hardly ever stopped talking; who was full of laughing and carrying-on and winning.

Sally stared hard at the green bleeps. If they were to stop . . . Sally didn't dare to think any further.

She watched her mother take Thalia's limp hand, telling her that they would soon be in to see her again, and saw Thalia's hand fall back on to the cover when her mother let go of it.

Mr Nisbet was standing at the nursing station talking to Narg. Sally followed her mother along the corridor towards them. In a way she hadn't seen Thalia at all. Sally knew that all Thalia would want to know about would be Tarquin. If she had been able to hear them, she would be certain that they hadn't mentioned Tarquin because he had been hurt.

"I've left my gloves," Sally said. "Better go back for them," and, before her mother had time to stop her, Sally was racing back to Thalia. She paused by Thalia's bed. In the dim light there was only the pulse of the monitor and Thalia lying so clean and so still.

"Listen," Sally said. "Tarquin is fine. He only scratched his leg and scraped his shoulder. He is totally, absolutely, all right. And the sooner you wake up, the sooner you'll be riding him again."

Thalia gave no sign of having heard her. For a furious second Sally wanted to get hold of Thalia and shake her free from the tube and the bleeps.

But that was impossible. You couldn't do that.

Suddenly Sally remembered the wisp of Tarquin's mane and her unicorn. They were still in her pocket. Hurriedly, Sally offered them to Thalia.

"They're to bring you magic," she said urgently. "A bit of Tarquin's mane and the unicorn."

Thalia's face showed no sign of life but slowly her right hand lifted from the bed cover, her palm turned towards Sally. Carefully Sally laid the wisp of roan hairs and the shimmering unicorn into the centre of Thalia's hand.

"Take care of them," she warned, and Thalia closed her hand over them, holding them safely.

"Are you still here?" demanded a sharp, nurse-voice.

"Going," said Sally. "Forgot my gloves."

"What were you doing?"

"Giving Thalia my unicorn," admitted Sally, expecting the nurse to pounce on Thalia and take it away from her.

The nurse looked quickly at Thalia and saw she was clasping something in her hand. "She took it from you?" she demanded in quite a different tone of voice.

"Oh, that is good. Very good indeed! That's great."

Sally escaped into the corridor brightness. Her mother, Narg and Mr Nisbet were still standing together, not chatting but talking seriously. As Sally ran towards them, bursting to tell them about Thalia, she heard Mr Nisbet saying, "So I MUST fly out to Washington later tonight. There is no way I can miss the conference. I can't bear to leave her like this. I shall keep on phoning the hospital until I hear she's regained consciousness. I'll be back for a visit just as soon as I can manage it. Terrible business. If only she would keep away from these dangerous horses. As you know I've made the arrangements. It will be collected. I'm giving you no details just in case Thalia manages to wheedle anything out of you."

"Well, I've told you what I think about it," said Narg, glaring at Mr Nisbet.

"About what?" Sally demanded but no one was listening to her.

Chapter Six

Next morning, Sally woke suddenly. She sat bolt upright, certain she could hear Tarquin neighing, which was impossible because her bedroom was at the very top of the stairs, too far from the stables for any pony noises to reach her.

Straining her ears, Sally listened intently. Again she heard Tarquin's screaming whinny but this time she could hear the engine of a heavy vehicle being driven towards the avenue. Tarquin called again; a long whinny of desperation.

Sally threw herself out of bed, scrabbled into her clothes, hurtled downstairs and out into the cold, early morning dark.

"Tarquin! Tarquin!" she shouted as she raced to the stables.

Willow's head reached over the half-door as she strained against it, trying to burst it open. She greeted Sally with sharp snorts through her wide nostrils, then swung away to circle her box and clatter her front feet against the box door.

Stumbling in her speed to reach the looseboxes, Sally raced across the yard.

"Tarquin," she yelled frantically. "Tarquin!" but Tarquin's box was empty; the door bolted.

For a second Sally gripped the bottom half of the door and stared into the dark of the box, as if Tarquin had been kitten-sized and she might have over-looked him, but nothing changed. The box was empty.

Paying no attention to Willow, Sally tore back to Kestrels. Tarquin must have been in the horsebox that she had heard. Someone had stolen him.

"Tarquin's gone!" Sally cried, finding her parents in the kitchen drinking tea.

"Tarquin's gone!" she cried again. "He's been stolen. I heard a horsebox. Quick! Come on, quick! Quick! Get the car. Someone may remember seeing him. But we've got to go now. At once!"

Gradually, Sally realized that her parents did not seem surprised or shocked.

"Mr Nisbet told Narg and me at the hospital," her mother said, when Sally paused for breath. "He said Tarquin was far too dangerous for Thalia to go on riding him and, to make quite certain she could not ride him, he'd arranged for a dealer to collect him and keep Tarquin in his yard."

Sally's jaw dropped open. She could not believe what her mother was saying.

"There really was nothing we could do," said Mr Lorimer. "And I must say I can see the man's point of view. If it had been you . . ."

"He had no right to touch Thalia's pony. Tarquin's not dangerous. It was the tarpaulin. And Mr Nisbet bashing his horn."

"Well, it's done now," stated Mr Lorimer.

"Of course it's not," cried Sally. "We must find him and bring him home. What will Thalia say? She'll die, that's what she'll do; die if we don't find him."

"Oh, Sally," began her mother.

"Does Narg know where he is?"

"No. He wouldn't tell her either," said Mrs Lorimer, as Sally made a dash for the phone.

"No, I do not!" said Narg. "Only what he told us last night. Wouldn't wait, wouldn't listen to me. Always been a whizz kid by his way of thinking. Pathetic, I call it."

"And how's Thalia?" Sally demanded; already in her mind she was galloping to Mr Frazer's, to see if Tarquin was there.

"I'm going to the hospital now. I phoned a few minutes ago and she's still unconscious. She'll be so upset when she finds out that Tarquin has gone. Don't know what she'll do. But I couldn't get him to change his mind."

Sally gobbled toast to satisfy her mother, then hurried out, Fen shadowing her heels. She gave Willow a drink and then a small

74

feed of pony nuts, and an armful of hay to munch while she brushed her down.

There was no Tarquin in the next box, no familiar sound of hoofs on stone as he ranged round his box; no intelligent roan head watching as Sally led Willow out. Sally swallowed the hard lump in her throat. She had to find Tarquin.

Sally rode down to the shore and galloped to the riding school, Fen loping at Willow's side. Mr Frazer's was the only dealer's yard in the district and Sally felt certain that Mr Nisbet must have sent Tarquin there.

There was no sign of Martine. A smartly turned-out lady was mounting a clipped hunter, a boy was wheeling a barrow to the dungheap and another girl was leading four rough ponies across the yard.

"Is Martine about?" Sally asked her.

"Caught a virus," the girl said. "She's to stay in bed."

"Mr Frazer?" Sally asked desperately.

"In his office doing the books. I wouldn't disturb him if I were you. Unless it's really, really urgent."

"Couldn't be more urgent. Got to find out," Sally thought, as she watched the girl sort out the halter ropes and march across the yard towing the ponies behind her as if they were on wheels.

"You must ask him," Sally told herself. "Must."

Holding Willow by the buckle of her reins Sally could just reach the office door. She knocked timidly, but there was no reply. "It's to find Tarquin," Sally told herself and, spotting a brass door knocker high up on the door, she stood on tiptoe and banged it hard again and again.

The door swung open and Mr Frazer stood there.

"I have told you, not when I'm checking the VAT—" he began, but stopped when he saw that it was not one of his staff.

"I'm sorry," said Sally. "I didn't know. Thalia is still unconscious and someone has taken her pony."

"What?" roared Mr Frazer. "What are you talking about?"

"About Thalia's pony—" began Sally, but Mr Frazer did not want an answer.

"Go!" he commanded.

"But did you?" insisted Sally. "Did you come to Kestrels this morning and take Tarquin?"

"NO!" thundered Mr Frazer and slammed the door in Sally's face.

Sally waited a moment to let her churned-up feelings settle.

"Guess he really doesn't know anything about Tarquin," she said to Willow as she remounted and rode across the yard, not having any idea what to do next.

The sliding doors at either end of the indoor school had been pushed open. Inside, the jumps were still arranged in the course Sally had jumped with Hannah. That was before the crash. Sally felt misery settling like a wet rug over her shoulders. She thought of Tarquin, standing in a horsebox, being driven further and further away; of Thalia, still unconscious.

"What would Thalia do?" Sally asked herself. "If Thalia were here, what would she do? She'd jump, Thalia would have a jump round."

Sally gazed at the jumps and swallowed hard.

"Well? Why not? Prove that it wasn't a fluke; that Willow can showjump. Right," Sally said aloud and, glancing quickly round to make sure that there was no one watching, she rode into the indoor school. Straightening her shoulders, Sally blotted out the nervous, twittering voices that filled her head. She would ride the way Thalia rode. "Straight on."

Sally trotted Willow in schooling circles and then cantered. As she rode, it came to Sally almost without thinking that it mattered that she should jump well; should not be afraid; that somehow it mattered to Thalia and to Tarquin.

With the course she was to jump clear in her mind, Sally rode Willow at the first jump. Normally when Sally jumped her mind was cold and clenched, but today was different. She was thinking about take-offs and landings, being ready for the next jump; going fast for spreads and slower for height.

Willow, feeling her rider's determination, made nothing of the first three jumps.

She cleared the double with neat-hoofed accuracy and, when she had popped over the next two jumps, she was ready to turn and face the last jump – the red-and-white wall.

Suddenly Sally realized that the wall had been raised. "Must stop Willow jumping," zipped through her mind. But only for a second. "Thalia would jump," and instantly she was riding Willow at the wall.

Willow checked, as she too realized the height of the wall.

"On you go," cried Sally, urging Willow on with seat and heels.

Willow rose in a perfect arc and landed far out. Sally, clapping her neck and praising her pony, galloped on out of the indoor school with the applause of the invisible spectators filling her head.

"We did it," Sally cried. "No one to make us. We did it ourselves," and, for a second, she was overflowing with glory before the thought of Thalia in hospital and Tarquin stolen came back to her.

Narg was in the kitchen when Sally got back to Kestrels.

"And where have you been?" asked Mrs Lorimer sharply.

"Mr Frazer's. Tarquin's not there."

"And lying so flat," said Narg going on, speaking to Sally's mother. "They told me not to cry when I was with her, in case she knew, but I couldn't help it. Don't think she knew, but you can't tell when she's like this. They're worried about her. Asked me to come back this afternoon and bring Sally with me."

"You knew Thalia's father was going to steal Tarquin? You knew, didn't you?" Sally accused Narg.

"Oh, he went on and on about it. Dangerous, mad pony. How we must get rid of him. I told him it would break her heart, but he only said, 'Better her heart than her head.' Couldn't stop him. He'd arranged for some stable to come and collect Tarquin. Wouldn't tell me any more than that. Said if I didn't know Thalia couldn't know. And what could I have done?"

"You could have told me," stated Sally. "We could have found some way of hiding Tarquin; some way of following the horsebox. You should have *made* him tell you!"

Mrs Lorimer gave Sally a hard look.

"Enough," she said. "How will you get to the hospital? Rob has got the car. I'll look up the times of the buses."

"Buses," snorted Narg, pulling herself together, "I've got my bike and Thalia's crash lid for Sally."

Chapter Seven

Clinging tightly to Narg's broad, wax-jacketed back, Sally was hurtled through barricades of traffic as Narg rode her motorbike with the obsession of Mr Toad.

She parked close to the hospital, totally ignoring the sign that said *Ambulances Only*, and rushed Sally into a lift and up to the Intensive Care Unit.

"Any change, Doctor?" she challenged the first doctor they met.

The doctor shook his head, recognizing Narg.

"Is this Sally, Thalia's friend?" he asked,

smiling at Sally. "Now, tell me exactly what happened when Thalia took your little charm from you."

"I told her that Tarquin wasn't hurt, then I gave her my unicorn and a few hairs from Tarquin's mane."

"Did you put them in her hand?"

"Yes," said Sally. "She opened her hand. I gave them to her and she closed her fingers round them."

"You're sure? You didn't fold her hand over them?"

"Sure."

"Good. Now, perhaps if you both sit with Thalia for ten minutes or so, and then we'll leave Sally alone with her."

Thalia lay motionless on her bed. The bleep and zigzag lines chased each other over the monitor screen. Narg's voice, telling Thalia that they had come to see her, spoke to itself.

Sally sat on the edge of the hospital chair, her hands tucked under her legs, waiting for Narg to go; waiting to be left alone with Thalia so she could tell her what had happened; so she could make her wake up.

"I'll leave you," said Narg at last. "Don't wait too long. I'll be at the nursing station along the corridor."

She got to her feet and marched out of the open door, wiping her eyes as she went.

Sally took a deep breath and knelt down by the head of the bed.

"It's me. Sally," she said, as loudly as she dared. "Now listen. Something dreadful has happened. Are you listening? Your flippin' father has nobbled Tarquin. I think he has sold him. Tarquin has gone! No one knows where he is. You must come and help me find him. Now wake up. Pull yourself together. We've got to find him."

Sally sat back on her heels and stared at Thalia. "Wake up!" she repeated, fixing all her will on Thalia. "Oh wake up!"

The bleep and the zigzag pulsed across the screen. Along the corridor a nurse was pushing a trolley but, in Thalia's room, time had stopped. She lay totally without movement.

"Thalia, please, please wake up. It's no use – I can't find Tarquin on my own."

As Sally stared helplessly, Thalia's hand

suddenly opened and the unicorn fell on to the cover. She searched for it with her hand, found it again and closed her fingers safely over it. A noise that was half joy, half sorrow burst out of Sally.

"You moved," she cried. "You knew you had dropped the unicorn. Now you've got to hurry up. Lift your other arm. Come on. We won't find Tarquin if all you can do is lift one hand."

Very slowly Thalia moved her other arm.

"You did it!" gasped Sally. "If you can hear me, lift the hand with the unicorn in it."

Thalia did as she was told.

"Tarquin is not at Mr Frazer's. I'm going to tell all the pony people I can think of to keep their ears and eyes open for any sign of Tarquin and—"

"Time to go now," said a nurse, coming in to see how Sally was getting on. "Say bye-bye to her."

Thalia lifted her arm and waved goodbye to Sally.

"Did you see that?" exclaimed the nurse. "She's coming round. Wait till I get Sister," and the nurse bustled away making small sounds of delight.

"Don't think you can go unconscious again," Sally warned Thalia. "You've got to get out of here at once."

Later that afternoon, when Sally went down to the field to bring Willow in, she was standing by the gate. She whinnied when she saw Sally; tearing up and down the hedge at a battering trot, her New Zealand rug plastered with mud where she had been rolling.

Sally held out sliced carrot and settled the halter over Willow's head. On their way back to the stables Willow pulled and barged wanting to charge back in case Tarquin should be there.

"He's not," warned Sally, as Willow plunged at the length of her rope, pulling Sally along behind her.

In the stable yard Willow shrieked through trumpeting nostrils. But there was no reply. She listened for a moment – head high, eyes wild, neighed once more, then, accepting that Tarquin was not there, she sighed, deflated and followed Sally quietly into her box.

"But Thalia will soon be OK," Sally told her, as she struggled to unbuckle the mud-caked rug. "And then we'll find him. It won't be long before he's home again."

Sally, helped by Emma, phoned round all the pony people who knew Tarquin. Most of them had heard about Thalia's accident; they'd sent cards and flowers to the hospital, but none of them knew anything about Tarquin.

"Of course I'll keep looking," Mrs Blair promised. "A pony with a jump in it like Tarquin doesn't vanish into thin air. Tell Thalia not to upset herself. We'll find him. The Pony Club needs him. I'm sure we can persuade her father to change his mind."

Mr Lorimer phoned Mr Frazer who seemed to have calmed down and assured Mr Lorimer that he knew nothing about Tarquin and would let him know if he heard anything. "Bit of a rogue pony," he added. "But the child has always seemed capable enough to me."

Sally wrote the last bit down so she would remember to tell Thalia.

Simon Knowles, who had two ponies – Clover, who had once been a riding-school pony, and Zodiac, an expensive eventing pony – said he would ask a farmer he knew to keep a look-out for Tarquin at the market.

The phone rang at seven o'clock the next evening.

"This place," said Mr Lorimer, tripping over Meg, "is turning into a telephone exchange," but when he answered it, it was Narg to tell them that she was in the hospital and that Thalia was fully conscious again.

"Oh, wonderful news!" he said, hardly having time to speak before his wife grabbed the phone from him.

"Is she really all right?" Mrs Lorimer demanded.

"Seems blooming," Narg replied, and Mrs Lorimer blew her nose hard on a tissue supplied by Jamie.

When Sally, Jamie and their mother visited Sally the next afternoon she was out of intensive care and in a ward with two other girls.

"Hi!" Thalia yelled, waving wildly from her bed, her yellow hair flaming round her head. "I'm here. Have you found Tarquin?"

"Lovely to see you alive again," said Mrs Lorimer, kissing Thalia. "You look perfectly restored."

"Have you found him?" Thalia demanded as she dodged Mrs Lorimer's kiss. "If I could get out of here I'd find him. You've got to get a move on. He could be anywhere by now. I hate my father. I really hate him. How could anyone do such a filthy, rotten thing?"

"I expect he was worried about you," suggested Mrs Lorimer. "I would be if I'd seen Sally thrown off in the middle of traffic."

"I was not thrown off!" exclaimed Thalia. "Tarquin came down with me. If they'd take this blooming tube out of my nose I could get out of here and start looking for him. He *is* my pony, you know."

A passing nurse looked in and warned them not to excite Thalia.

"Excite me!" cried Thalia. "I am not excited. I am in the depths of despair. What have you done to find him? Flippin' nothing."

Sally told Thalia what she had done, but Thalia was not impressed.

"So what are you going to do tomorrow? Where are you going to look tomorrow?"

"Now that I've brought you back to consciousness—" retorted Sally.

"She's going to get her hair cut," said Mrs Lorimer. "And the day after next is Monday. The Christmas holidays are over and she goes back to school."

Sally stared at her mother in shocked surprise for, of course, she had known that school started again on Monday, she just had not realized that Monday was so soon.

"And who is going to look for Tarquin when I'm in prison here and Sally's in prison at school?"

Before they left the hospital Thalia gave the unicorn back to Sally.

"It's not safe here," she said. "You have no idea how many times they've tried to take it away from me. And someone has stolen Tarquin's hair!"

Sally walked backwards down the corridor. She could still see Thalia reflected in one of the mirrors. She looked small and alone, surrounded by get-well cards pinned to the wall. Three were from her mother.

After tea Sally went down to the stables to be with Willow for a bit.

"You miss him, don't you?" Sally said, going into the box, leaning against her pony, burying her face into the warm, good smell of Willow's mane. "They don't care. Not enough. If they did, we'd stop everything. Do nothing but look, until we found Tarquin."

Willow butted Sally impatiently. She knew there were titbits in Sally's pocket.

"The only person who knows where he is, is Thalia's filthy father." Sally stopped talking and heard what she had said. "Thalia's father. I'll ask him. I'll write to him."

Sally whirled round, said goodnight to Willow, carefully bolted the box door, then ran to Kestrels. She flung herself up the broad staircase and clambered up the stairs to her room. She found notepaper and envelopes. They were decorated with dream ponies with long, waving manes. Sally did not think Mr Nisbet would appreciate them, but it was all she had.

She took the notepaper over to the window, placed her unicorn carefully on the windowsill. She knelt in front of the window seat and, with her good fountain pen that she hardly ever used, she started to write. Her address and the date were easy but, after that, she could not think what to say. An author who had visited their school had told them that they must write from their hearts. Sally drew in a deep breath and wrote from her heart.

"Dear Mr Nisbet," she wrote,

I think you are the most foul, beastly, rotten man. Where is Tarquin? Thalia is unconscious and you have stolen her pony. Thalia loves Tarquin and they are brilliant showjumpers. And you did this! Please, please, please let Thalia know where he is.

With hate,
Sally Lorimer

Sally folded the letter, and quickly, before she could have second thoughts about "with hate", she crammed it into an envelope and sealed it.

Next morning she rode over to Narg's and persuaded Narg to give her Mr Nisbet's Washington address. She wrote URGENT in large, red letters on the envelope before she posted it airmail to America.

Chapter Eight

Thalia got out of hospital ten days after the accident. They had wanted to make absolutely sure she had not damaged her head.

"Brutal," she said, clambering into Mr Lorimer's car, avoiding Narg's helping hands and Sally's watching.

"I shall hang my real, true, ancient, beloved hat above my bed and, even if I'm only looking at ponies, I shall wear my new hat, the one your dad bought for me."

Narg sat in the front with Mr Lorimer; Sally and Thalia in the back so they could talk together without being overheard.

"I wrote to your father. Couldn't tell you in hospital, not with all your visitors. I finished off, 'with hate'. But he hasn't replied."

"I'd have put 'HATE, HATE, HATE'. He won't write. Never does. I kid myself he can't."

"But the good news is Martine's back. She had flu. Started today because Saturday's their busy day."

"We'll go round this afternoon," stated Thalia.

Narg was difficult. She thought Thalia should rest.

"But I am completely cured."

Narg considered.

"I am quite all right. Honestly."

"Promise me you won't ride for another week?"

"Only Willow?"

"Not ride at all," insisted Narg. "Doctor warned me that you were not to ride until he'd seen you again."

"Solemn vow," swore Thalia. "Unless it is a matter of life and death."

"Be home before dark," said Narg.

Sally rode Willow slowly along the shore to the riding school while Thalia dawdled at her side.

Martine was in the yard watching a group of six adults riding out. As soon as she saw Thalia she ran to her and hugged her.

"Oh, I am so pleased to see you. Been hearing the most hair-raising accounts of your accident."

"Do you know where Tarquin is?" Thalia demanded, escaping from Martine's embrace. "Did no one see him being driven away?"

"Mr Frazer knows nothing. Not a whisper of a roan pony for sale. The only one I can think of is Andy Moore. Remember he had his eye on Tarquin at the Christmas Show?"

Thalia nodded. She remembered the hairy man who had wanted to buy Tarquin perfectly well, and yet it was ages ago; it had been about a week before the accident.

"I phoned him up. He said he knew nothing about a roan pony. But you never know with Andy. If you want to be sure about anything, you have to go to his yard in Radford and look for yourself."

"We'll go tomorrow," said Thalia.

"Sorry, but I can't take you. I'm working," said Martine.

"And Dad's at a library conference thing," said Sally.

"We'll bus it to Radford," said Thalia. "I've been before with Narg."

"Make sure your parents approve," warned Martine, then, turning to Sally, she asked her if she would like a jump round in the indoor school.

"Yes, please," said Sally beaming, then remembered that Thalia had no pony and added, "that's if Thalia doesn't mind."

"Idiot. Of course I don't," muttered Thalia, not looking at Sally.

Thalia and Martine watched while Sally rode Willow in schooling circles. Martine told Sally the course she was to jump and made her repeat it until she really knew it.

"Now remember: ride it as a course, not single jumps."

Sally nodded, concentrating hard; then,

easing Willow into a canter she rode at the first jump.

The jumps unrolled beneath her as neatly as the different movements had fitted together when she had ridden the dressage test in the Pony Club one-day event.

"Well done," Martine praised.

"You have improved," said Thalia. "It's when you're in a competition that you make such a muck of things."

"A thing of the past?" suggested Martine. "Not at Broughton?"

"I *must* find Tarquin before Broughton Show," interrupted Thalia.

"You will," promised Martine. "Now we're both on the move again we'll find him. You'll jump at Broughton. You're bound to find Tarquin. He's your pony."

Next morning, Ben, Sally and Thalia were standing at the bus stop for Radford. Mrs Lorimer and Narg had both said a definite "No" to the idea of Sally and Thalia going to Andy Moore's stables by themselves. Ben had taken pity on them.

It was raining when they reached Radford.

"You know the way?" Ben asked.

Thalia showed him the map Martine had drawn for them.

"We're here," Thalia pointed out, as the rain blurred the felt-tipped lines. "We go along this street, turn right and on until we reach the stables."

"Right," said Ben. "I'm going in here for a coffee or two, so you'll find me here when you come back with the horse. Joke! Ha ha!" and he pushed open a café door, taking a book out of his pocket as he did so.

As Sally and Thalia ran down the street between the high, red sandstone buildings and modern shops the rain grew heavier and more of Martine's map flowed away every time they looked at it.

"But that can't be it. It's in the middle of the town," stated Sally, gazing up at a stone archway that led off the street.

"Must be," said Thalia. "That's what it says: *Andrew Moore. Livery Stables*! I'm so sick I could die," she said. "Tarquin MUST be here," and she ran full speed into the stable yard.

99

It was a large, uncared-for yard with a modern bungalow at one end. Rows of shoddy stabling surrounded the other three sides. Heads appeared over half-doors, some shaggy pony heads, some fine-skinned thoroughbreds, some workaday horses. But there was no roan pony. Tarquin was not there.

"Perhaps you've missed him?" suggested Sally.

"Some chance!" said Thalia. "Me? Miss Tarquin!" but she went round again more slowly than the first time, her gaze glossing over greys and bays, skewbalds and chestnuts.

"Better find the man and ask," said Thalia in a flat voice.

"He might have some in a field," suggested Sally.

"Field near a supermarket?" scorned Thalia.

The door of the bungalow opened and a man strode into the yard. It was Andy Moore, the same man who had wanted to buy Tarquin at the Christmas Show.

"You looking for something?" said

Andy Moore. "Private property, you're on. Here, I know you, Blondie. Saw you at Frazer's show. Pony with a bit of go in him, that right? You come to see me about selling him? Eh?"

"Bloomin' not," said Thalia indignantly. "We want to know if you have him."

"Ah, like I said. Your dad heard the rustle of the money, has he?"

"If Tarquin is here, I want to buy him back."

"Dare say you do. I get plenty of that these days. Parents buy ponies for the youngsters, then can't afford to keep them. Send the ponies to me to be sold and then you kids come howling to me, wanting to buy them back with ten pounds clutched in your hands!"

"I can't see him here—" Thalia began.

"Then that's it, isn't it? He's not here, so get off with you. NOW! And don't let me see you hanging about here again. Right?"

Thalia and Sally walked smartly out of the yard. There was no high, echoing whinny that could only have been Tarquin to call them back.

Ben had drunk five cups of coffee and had finished his book. He was not too happy.

They stood at the bus stop in the pouring rain. They waited and waited. It was the Sunday service and the bus took nearly an hour to arrive. Thalia stayed on the bus and went straight home to Narg's. When Ben and Sally got home to Kestrels, Sally's mother fussed her into a hot bath and bed with a book. Sally's eyes closed after half a page. She woke two hours later, her head filled with the one thought that they had not found Tarquin and it was Broughton Show next Saturday.

Next Wednesday, Sally's school had a teacher-training holiday. Thalia was not to go back to school until next week. She was spending her time cycling round, checking fields and farms in case Tarquin should be there. On Wednesday they had lunch in Tarquin's loosebox – flasks of carrot and mushroom soup, cheese quiche and apples.

"This is the only place I'm happy. Least I can still smell him here," Thalia was saying, when there was the clatter of approaching hoofs and Simon Knowles, who was in the Pony Club, rode into the yard on Zodiac, his event pony, leading Clover, his ex-riding-school pony.

"Your mother told me you were here. I've asked her and she says it's O K."

"Asked her what?" demanded Thalia.

"If it would be all right for you to come with me. She phoned your Narg, and it is," said Simon, as he jumped to the ground. "I've brought Clover for you."

"What's O K?" asked Sally.

"I think," said Simon, almost exploding with his secret, "I think I know where Tarquin is!"

"Tell me!" screamed Thalia. "Tell me!"

"Do you know that house that used to be a church? New people moved in. Two boys about our age. At first they'd no ponies. Now they have two, and I'm sure one of them is Tarquin. I saw him in a field."

"Quick!" yelled Thalia. "Now. At once."

In seconds she had buttoned up her jacket, put on her hard, hard hat and was taking Clover from Simon.

"Come on. Hurry up," she shouted. "Oh, come on."

Sally tacked up Willow, her fingers fumbling with excitement as she pulled up Willow's girth. Simon knew Tarquin well. He couldn't possibly have made a mistake.

They reached the house after an hour's riding. It was a grey, stone house with a steeple and church windows. Its drive, padded with pine needles, was pitted with hoofprints.

Hardly pausing, Thalia trotted up to the house, dismounted and abandoned Clover. She raced up the steps and pressed her finger on the doorbell. The alarm of the bell rang through the house, but there was no answer.

"The stables are in a lane at the side of the house," said Simon as Thalia threw herself back into the saddle and led the way down a track to a cluster of portable stabling.

Hearing hoofs, a young woman wearing jeans and a brilliantly coloured sweater came out of the tack room.

"Hi," she called. "Nice to see you. Is this a getting-to-know-you visit or can I help you?"

Clover's trot changed to a canter as Thalia urged her on, pulling her to a halt, inches from the woman.

"Simon says you've got Tarquin," she accused. "He is my pony. My father had no right to sell him and you have no right to have him. You must give him back to me. He's mine."

"Steady on," said the woman. "Maybe you *think* I've got your pony?"

"He's a roan," said Thalia. "And a super showjumper. And he's mine."

"I really don't know what you're talking about. We do have a roan pony – Pepper – but he belongs to Ralph. And he certainly is not any kind of showjumper. See for yourself."

The woman walked round the side of the stabling. One loosebox was empty; a bay head looked out over the second door and, from the third box, a roan pony watched them intently.

It was not Tarquin. Nothing like Tarquin. It had a straggly mane, a thickset neck and a mean eye that showed a lot of white.

"Well," said Simon defensively. "I only saw him from a distance and he is roan and he is the same size."

Thalia stood digging the buckle of Clover's reins into her hand to stop herself crying. She had been so sure; had allowed herself to be too certain. For the first time she began to despair of *ever* finding Tarquin.

Chapter Nine

Mr Frazer's best horsebox, loaded with two bay show horses, one chestnut showjumper, all belonging to the Webster family, who stabled their horses with Mr Frazer, and Willow, sped along the motorway to Broughton. Martine was at the wheel. Thalia and Sally stared silently through the windscreen. They were both wearing riding clothes.

"You never know," Thalia had insisted. "Tarquin might be at Broughton Show. Whoever has him will want to jump him and Broughton is the only show near here until the spring. And Mr Frazer has entered both of us."

Only Narg had been hard enough to tell her that it was all a nonsense; that the only thing to do was to wait for her father to return from Washington which should not be too long now, and ask him.

"All the same," Thalia had insisted, "you never know. Tarquin might be at Broughton. So I've got to be ready to jump him, just in case."

Sally had woken up knowing that today she was going to showjump Willow in a strange, indoor school. She had turned over and pressed her face into her pillow to shut out the day, before she thought of Thalia. Even if she fell off again it could not possibly be as bad as searching hopelessly for your lost pony.

Martine drove into the horsebox section of the car park. The Websters were waiting to take their horses. Thalia led Willow out of the box and helped Sally to tack her up.

"I can't leave the box here," Martine told them. "I've to take it across the road and park there. Can you two manage? Can you get Sally's number? I'll find you again before your class."

"Course we can manage," said Thalia. "I'll get my number too. Best to be ready. I really am sure that I'll find Tarquin here. I just know I will.

"When is the class?" Thalia asked as she tied 63 on to Sally's back, 71 on to herself.

"Half past eleven," said Sally, suddenly realizing that she would be in the ring in an hour's time.

"I'll come with you to the exercising bit and then I'll need to look for Tarquin."

"He might not be here," warned Sally, but Thalia paid no attention to her.

The exercising area was a large, uneven stretch of gravel. It was packed with horses and ponies and riders. Friends or family held up practice jumps, heavyweight hunters thundered round, and a woman riding side-saddle on her dapple grey Arab ignored all the noise and commotion, concentrating totally on her schooling.

"He must be here," Thalia muttered to herself. "All I've got to do is find him."

Willow tittupped along, her head high, eyes staring from her head, her ears twitching at the din of this madness of horses. She had never seen anything like it in her life. So many horses galloping and jumping, trotting and cantering; a massive surge of horses in such a small space. Willow stretched out her neck and whinnied long and loud.

A single whinny, high and brazen, answered her above the noise.

The blood drained from Thalia's face.

"It's—" she began but couldn't say any more.

Head down, she raged her way through the mass of horses, Willow and Sally fighting to stay with her.

Again Willow whinnied, and again the high, vibrant call answered her.

"Over this way," shouted Thalia, suddenly changing direction, quite unaware of a woman pulling her bay horse to a rearing halt to avoid riding her down.

At the far end of the exercising area a middle-aged woman, skinny as a bat's scream, was fighting to hold on to a roan pony's reins as he struggled to escape from her – tossing his head, scattering his mane, striking out with his forefeet.

"Tarquin!" Thalia screamed.

She threw herself straight at Tarquin, wrapping her arms round his neck, burying her face in his mane.

"Tarquin."

"Who the dickens are you?" demanded the stick woman. "Leave my pony alone."

"He's not your pony. He's Tarquin. My pony. Mine. They'd no right to take him away. He's my pony."

As Thalia spoke, she ran her hands over Tarquin's face – the flat cheekbone, the velvet soft muzzle – smoothing his forelock, pulling his ear through her hand. She had found Tarquin and nothing, nothing, nothing would ever make her let him go again.

Tarquin breathed over Thalia's face, with quick, sweet breath. He blew over her neck, pushed at her arm and rubbed his head against her shoulder. There was no doubt at all – he knew her, was as rapturous to find Thalia as she was to find him.

Willow wuffled her nostrils with puffs of sound, pulling to get to Tarquin, but Sally checked her. Thalia didn't want Willow pushing in.

The stick woman jerked at Tarquin's reins, pulling him away from Thalia.

"I can't imagine what this is all about," she said. "I've told you he is my pony."

"No! Tarquin is mine!"

"I've bought him for my daughter. He may have belonged to you or your parents at one time but he is most certainly mine now."

One of Thalia's hands was knotted into Tarquin's mane, her other arm was clutched protectively over his withers.

"He belongs to Thalia," Sally said. "If you bought him, it was all a mistake. Thalia's father had no right to sell him. You must give him back to us."

"Who are you children with?" demanded the woman. "Let go of him. My daughter will be jumping him in an hour. I can't stand here listening to such nonsense," and she tried to lead Tarquin away, but Thalia clung tightly to her pony, fighting to hold him back.

"Been looking for you everywhere—"

began Martine and then stopped. With once glance she took in the situation.

"Can I help?" she asked, sounding very much a responsible adult. "I know this pony. He should never have been sold. It was all a mistake. I'm sure when you hear the story you'll understand."

"You listen to me. My cheque is in the bank, I have the pony on trial. I have paid good money for this pony and, as far as I'm concerned, that is the end of the matter. Now kindly take this child away and talk some sense into her."

Sally held her breath, expecting Thalia to fight – kicking, clawing and spitting – to fight the woman with all her strength; to spring on to Tarquin, jump out of the exercise area and gallop away.

Martine put her arm round Thalia's shoulders.

"At least," she said to the woman, "let me know where you got him."

"Brookmead stables, near Ranley. Not that it is any of your business, nor will it make the slightest difference. The pony belongs to me."

For a moment Thalia waited, still holding on to Tarquin and then she let go. She turned away and, without looking back, was threading her way through the horses and riders.

Sally hurried after her, while Martine waited, still trying to persuade the woman to let them have Tarquin back.

Thalia marched on, leaving the exercise area behind her.

"Might as well watch the jumping," she muttered, without looking round at Sally.

They went into the vast indoor school, brash with electric light, loudspeakers and crowd. A wooden barricade divided the rows of seating from the ring. Thalia and Sally stood beside it.

"That's it," Thalia said. "Guess I'll never see—" but she couldn't finish the sentence. She laid her arms on the wooden barrier, buried her face in her hands and wept.

Sally stared at Thalia's back not knowing what to do. She couldn't tell Thalia that it would be all right because it didn't look as if it would be. She couldn't pretend that it would be easy to get Tarquin back again because it didn't look as if it would even be possible.

Sally stared at the ring not seeing ponies or riders: only Tarquin standing watching Thalia walking away from him.

Chapter Ten

Sally watched out for Martine at the entrance to the indoor arena. She was wondering if Martine would be able to find them there or if she should leave Thalia and look for her, when suddenly Thalia's father came through the entrance.

He stood, a little man in a smart, grey suit and highly polished shoes, looking weird and lost. In one hand he carried an expensive, leather briefcase and in the other he clutched a pony's reins. At the end of the reins a roan pony struggled to break free. Mr Nisbet paid absolutely no attention to it, seemed totally unaware that there was anything at the end of the reins – like a Zen monk leading a dragon.

"It's Tarquin," Sally yelled. "Thalia, it's Tarquin. It's your dad and he's got Tarquin!"

Sally grabbed Thalia's arm, pulling at her to turn her round.

"What?" said Thalia, rubbing her tear-stained face. "What?"

And then she saw her father, saw Tarquin.

With a scream of joy, Thalia rushed to her father.

"How did you find us?" she demanded, snatching Tarquin's reins from her father's hand. "Why did you sell him? He's my pony! *My* pony! What are you doing here? Have you bought him back? He's mine now, isn't he? Tell me he's mine?"

Mr Nisbet smoothed his thin, gingery hair with a nervous hand.

"Yes," he said. "He's yours."

Martine found them and listened too.

"Tarquin was never sold," explained Mr Nisbet. "He seemed to me to be a thoroughly dangerous animal. I had to get him well away in case you came out of hospital and started riding him again. One of my colleagues told me about Brookmead stables. Said it was one of the best, and far enough away to stop you tracking him down. So I sent him there. But he was not for sale. That woman who brought him here today had no right to do so. She said the stables had allowed her to bring Tarquin to see if her daughter could cope with him. They shouldn't have done that. I told them so when I got in touch with them this morning.

"So, my dear daughter, although you will not believe me, I was only doing what I thought would be best for you."

"You could have let us know what you were doing," Martine stated. "Saved a lot of misery."

"Hoped she might forget about the wretched beast. Didn't mean to cause all this agony."

"You're sure, sure, sure that Tarquin is mine again?"

"Absolutely," said her father. "For ever. I would not like to risk receiving any more fan letters – saw myself as others see me. Not too pleasant."

Sally busied herself sorting out strands of Willow's mane. She still felt guilty about "with hate".

"But it was all true," she muttered.

Martine began asking Mr Nisbet about his arrangements with Brookmead stables, whether she could take Tarquin back with them tonight. Thalia was intent on checking over Tarquin, whispering to him that he was safe, testing the miracle that he really had come home to her.

For a moment, no one was paying any attention to Sally. She sat astride Willow, full of beaming happiness.

"Number 63?" called the Tannoy. "Last call for Sally Lorimer, number 63."

Sally checked, her eyes flickering from side to side without moving her head. No one except herself had heard the announcement. She didn't need to jump. She could pretend she hadn't heard.

"Pretend to yourself?" asked the mocking voice in Sally's head. "Pretend you haven't heard when you know you have?

That's what you're here for – to jump."

"Shan't be a minute," Sally said, but no one bothered.

She turned Willow and rode her round to the entrance to the ring. "It'll be fun," she told her pony. "Like it was when we jumped in the indoor school by ourselves."

A steward ticked Sally's name off his list.

"Cutting it fine," he said. "Still, better late than never." Sally opened her mouth to explain but realized that there was no time, so she smiled at him instead – a smile that bubbled up from the very centre of her being and spread across her whole face – for Tarquin had been lost and was found.

"Know the course?"

Sally had never even thought about it – Tarquin was safe.

"Thought not," the steward said. "Well, listen carefully."

Sally concentrated hard as the steward explained the order of the jumps. She saw the course she was to ride as if there were a shimmering ribbon tracking along the ground and looping clear over the jumps – for Tarquin was saved.

She rode through the Start. The many times that Martine had told her that a pony must always be ridden in before you jump it had left no trace in Sally's mind. Willow would jump because Tarquin was safe; for the very joy that a small miracle had taken place, their own small miracle.

Willow pricked her ears, flicked her tail and galloped at the first jump. As they landed clear, Sally was already turning Willow towards a brush fence. Willow soared over it like a steeplechaser. Over an upright they went and galloped round the far end of the ring, on to the double.

Sally never hesitated. As Willow jumped the first part she was exactly right, a quick stride and they were clear over the second part – for Tarquin was safe. Tonight he would be back in his own box and tomorrow they would ride together, galloping over the wet sand.

They turned across the ring. Three more jumps, then over a white gate which trembled when Willow clipped it with her hind feet. Long after they had landed, Sally heard the gate fall to the ground. The gasp of the spectators followed her over the next jump, changing to a groan as she knocked down the last jump and galloped out of the ring.

"Eight faults for Sally Lorimer. Thank you, Sally."

And Sally wanted to stand up in her stirrups and shout – sharing her good news with them all – that Tarquin was safe.

It wasn't until she was out of the ring and riding back to join the others that Sally fully realized what had happened. She had jumped in an indoor arena without even thinking about it, when only a few weeks ago she had been completely fazed by the jumps and the lights. Today she had really showjumped and it had been terrific.

"Where have you been?" demanded Thalia.

"Jumping," said Sally.

"You pig! Why didn't you tell me?" and, even as she spoke, Thalia was tightening Tarquin's girth.

"Hat," she commanded as she mounted Tarquin and held her hand out to Martine for her hat.

Martine stepped towards Tarquin, ready-ing to prevent Thalia from riding him away. Then she stopped herself.

"Don't let him cart you," she warned, giving Thalia her hat. "Remember it's a few weeks since you rode him."

"What's she doing now?" asked Mr Nisbet. "Not going to jump, is she?"

But Thalia was away, trotting Tarquin towards the collecting ring.

There were three other children to jump before it was Thalia's turn. Tarquin pawed impatiently, half rearing, shaking his mane, hitching his quarters, while Thalia grinned around at everyone, filled with delight to be riding her own pony again.

She had two knock-downs.

When they announced the results, a boy on a grey was first, a fat girl with red cheeks on a black Fell pony was second, while Thalia and Sally had tied for third place.

"Due to a very tight schedule numbers 63 and 71 will toss for third place."

"Don't bother tossing a coin," Thalia told a steward when they rode back into the ring. "We're going to cut the rosettes in half, make them two-coloured. Specially for us."

Mr Nisbet was waiting impatiently. He had a plane to catch. "Well done, dear," he said to Thalia, then opened his briefcase and took out a large, lavishly illustrated book on horses.

"This is why I was chasing you. Wanted to give you this."

"Thank you!" exclaimed Thalia, leaping off Tarquin, taking the book and opening it. "Thank you very much indeed!"

"Well, must be off. Not much point in telling you to be careful when you can jump like that. Bye now."

Mr Nisbet turned and began to walk away, then he stopped suddenly, twinkled round and, dropping his briefcase, hugged Thalia to him. "I only wanted to be sure that you weren't riding a dangerous horse. That you wouldn't get hurt again."

"It's OK," said Thalia. "Honest it is. Now that I've got Tarquin back," but she clung to her father, not wanting to let him go.

"I'll see you again soon, I promise," and

in seconds Mr Nisbet, grey suit and thinning hair, was lost in the crowd.

"Promises, promises," said Thalia. "But it is a super book. I'll read it in Tarquin's box."

When the show was over Martine loaded up the horsebox with Willow, Tarquin and the Websters' horses and drove them back to Mr Frazer's. Kneeling on the cabin seat Thalia could just see Tarquin through the little window to the back of the box.

"You never know," she said, "when something absolutely wonderful or absolutely dreadful is going to happen."

Cradling her unicorn in her hand Sally agreed.

"There is always something lurking," said Martine.